THIS BLOOMSBURY BOOK

BELONGS TO

....

For Linda, Samantha and Amy — S.G.
For Emmet and Seamus — C.T.

First published in Great Britain in 2000 by Bloomsbury Publishing Plc
38 Soho Square, London, W1D 3HB
This paperback edition first published 2001

Text copyright © Sally Grindley 2000
Illustrations copyright © Carol Thompson 2000
The moral right of the author and illustrator has been asserted

A CIP catalogue record of this book is available from the British Library
ISBN 0 7475 5048 4 (Paperback)
ISBN 0 7475 4489 1 (Hardback)

Designed by Dawn Apperley

Printed in Hong Kong by South China Printing Co

1 3 5 7 9 10 8 6 4 2

A New Room for William

for hire

Sally Grindley and Carol Thompson

BLOOMSBURY
CHILDREN'S
BOOKS

William walked into his room in the new house and pulled a face.

"But I like my old room," he said. His old room had pictures on the walls and shelves crammed with toys. His old room had a soft red carpet and bright yellow curtains. This room was bare apart from his bed and a pile of boxes.

"Just wait and see," said Mum. "When we've finished in here you'll love it."

William looked out of the window. From his old room he could see his climbing frame. From his old room he could see the place where Dad let him dig. All he could see from this room was a tangle of weeds and a big old tree. A boy waved at him from next door. William ducked down below the window sill.

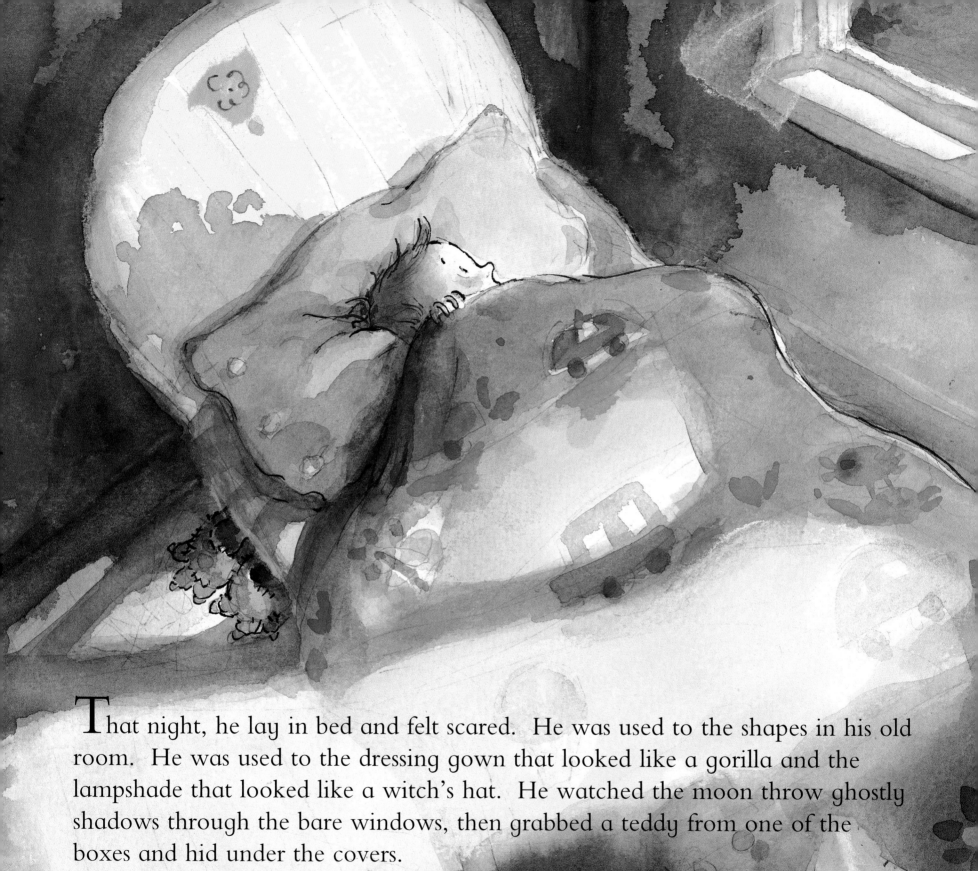

That night, he lay in bed and felt scared. He was used to the shapes in his old room. He was used to the dressing gown that looked like a gorilla and the lampshade that looked like a witch's hat. He watched the moon throw ghostly shadows through the bare windows, then grabbed a teddy from one of the boxes and hid under the covers.

"I want to go back to my old room in our old house," he cried, when Mum came to see if he was all right.

The next day, Mum took William shopping.

"Let's choose some wallpaper for your room," she said.

"I want the same paper I had in my old room," said William.

"That's fine," said Mum. "But look anyway. You might find one you like better."

William looked and found the paper that he'd had in his old room. He was about to choose it, when he saw a dinosaur staring at him from one of the papers. William liked dinosaurs.

"This one," he said suddenly. "I like this one."

When they went home, William rushed upstairs to his room and began to scrabble through one of the boxes.

He pulled out a model dinosaur, and another, and another, then stood them in a line on the window sill. The boy next door waved at him again. William waved back shyly and jumped his dinosaurs around.

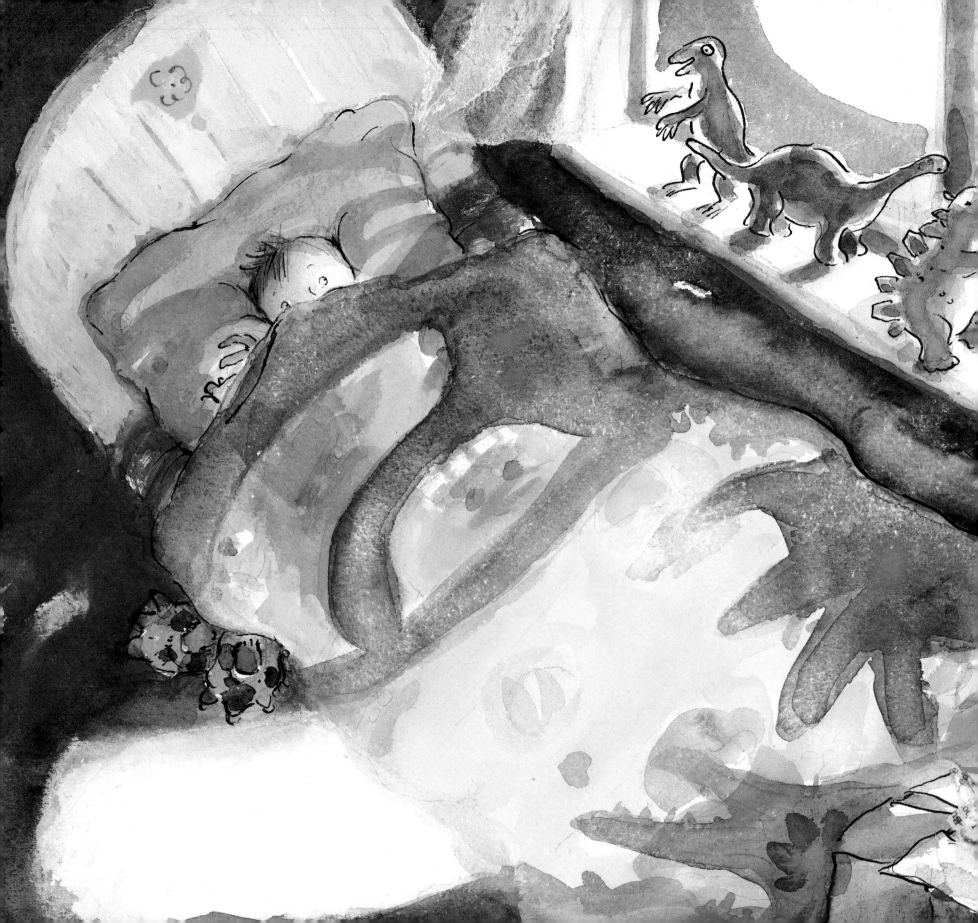

That night, William watched the moon throw ghostly shadows through the bare windows, and turned them all into dinosaurs.

"When will my new room be ready?" he asked, when Mum came to see if he was all right.

"I'll make a start in the morning," said Mum, "and you can help."

William woke bright and early.

"Can we start now?" he asked, as soon as he'd jumped out of bed.

"Can we start now?" he asked, as soon as he'd finished breakfast.

Mum let him stir the wallpaper paste – "Yuck! It's all slimy!" Then he held the ladder while Mum climbed up.

"Keep it steady, William!" she said.

Little by little, William's room
began to change, as more and
more dinosaurs covered the walls.
"They're chasing each other,
Mum!" cried William, and he ran
round the room pretending to be a
dinosaur.

Then he ran down to the garden and gallumphed along the garden path.

"GRRR!" he growled. "I'm a fierce dinosaur."

"RARRR!" came a voice. "I'm an even fiercer dinosaur."

Sitting in the big old tree was Tom, the boy from next door.

"Hello," said Tom. "You're new."

"I'm having a new room," said William proudly.

"Can I see it?" asked Tom.

"It's not finished yet," said William.

grrrr

William climbed the tree and sat next to Tom.

"We share this tree," said Tom. "Some of it's in my garden and some of it's in yours."

William looked down into Tom's garden. There was a climbing frame, just like the one he'd had at his old house. For a moment he felt sad again.

"We had to leave my climbing frame behind," he said.

"Let's go on mine," said Tom.

William clambered and scrambled and chased his new friend. What did it matter that this climbing frame was in Tom's garden and not his? Climbing frames were only fun if you had someone to play with, and he hadn't had a friend next door at his old house.

Suddenly, Mum opened a window and called down to him, "William, come and see your room now."

"Come on, Tom," said William excitedly. "Come and see my new room."

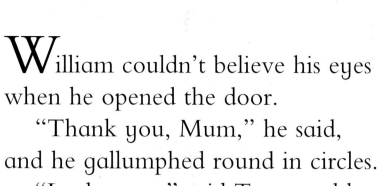

William couldn't believe his eyes when he opened the door.

"Thank you, Mum," he said, and he gallumphed round in circles.

"Lucky you," said Tom, and he gallumphed round behind him.

That night, William snuggled down with his teddy and looked round his new room. The moon shone brightly through the new curtains and picked out a Tyrannosaurus rex chasing a Stegosaurus. William smiled.

When Mum came in to see if he was all right, he said, "Will Dad let me choose the paper for my room at his new house?"

"I'm sure he will," said Mum. "Sleep tight now."

And William did.

Acclaim for *A New Room for William*

'Sally Grindley excels in stories that extend a child's emotional experience without becoming sentimental or precious' *The Scotsman*

Enjoy more great picture books from Bloomsbury ...

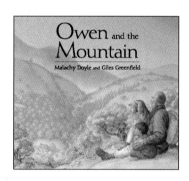

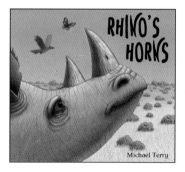

Owen and the Mountain
Malachy Doyle & Giles Greenfield

Be Good, Gordon
Angela McAllister & Tim Archbold

Rhino's Horns
Michael Terry

Eugene the Plane-Spotter
Katherine Lodge